Caitlin Hicks

Joey Barontini

Marissa Cruz

Tobey Diggs

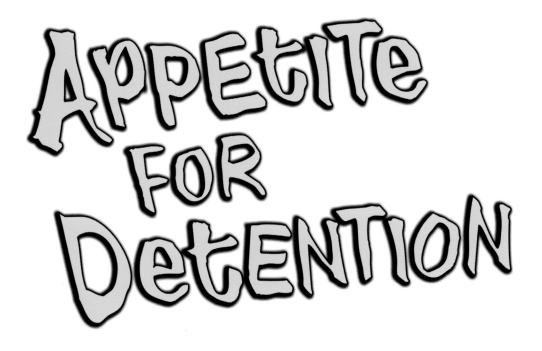

Appetite for Detention

Sloane Tanen

Photographed by **Stefan Hagen**

BLOOMSBURY

For Bebe, Coco, Harry, and Jesse

Copyright © 2008 by Sloane Tanen
Photographs copyright © 2008 by Stefan Hagen

Typeset in Stone Sans ITC
Book design by Donna Mark

Published by Bloomsbury U.S.A. Children's Books
175 Fifth Avenue, New York, New York 10010
Distributed to the trade by Macmillan

Library of Congress Cataloging-in-Publication Data
Tanen, Sloane.
Appetite for detention / Sloane Tanen ; photographed by Stefan Hagen. — 1st U.S. ed.
        p.   cm.
Summary: Text and photographs featuring pipe-cleaner chickens illustrate
experiences of a typical cross-section of teens, including coping with
out-of-control parents, stress pimples, weight problems, and trying to fit in.
ISBN-13: 978-1-59990-075-9 • ISBN-10: 1-59990-075-0 (hardcover)
[1. Interpersonal relations—Fiction. 2. High schools—Fiction. 3. Schools—Fiction.]
I. Hagen, Stefan, ill. II. Title.
PZ7.T16136Whe 2008   [Fic]—dc22   2007050831

First U.S. Edition 2008
Printed in China
1 3 5 7 9 10 8 6 4 2

All papers used by Bloomsbury USA are natural, recyclable products
made from wood grown in well-managed forests. The manufacturing processes
conform to the environmental regulations of the country of origin.

Also by Sloane Tanen

FOR ADULTS

Bitter with Baggage Seeks Same: The Life and Times of Some Chickens
Going for the Bronze: Still Bitter, More Baggage
Hatched! The Big Push from Pregnancy to Motherhood

FOR CHILDREN

Where Is Coco Going?
Coco All Year Round
C Is for Coco
Coco Counts

Professional highlights: $135.00
Juicy Couture handbag: $240.00
Knowing you'll be the prettiest girl in school:
Priceless

Joey liked fashion, not football. His father would
have to live out his thwarted teenage dreams through
someone else. Maybe his baby brother Tony . . .
but that wasn't looking too likely either.

Marissa had fainted. Was it nerves about going back to school, her strict 250-calorie-a-day diet, or toxic shock from the tampon she'd finally figured out how to use?

Edgar wasn't a skater, a punk, a jock, a geek, or a nerd.

He was just depressed, and he hadn't found that clique yet.

Andrew's looming bar mitzvah represented his two greatest fears:
public speaking and his parents finding out that he wasn't popular.
Unfortunately, the odds of him successfully addressing a crowd
(in Hebrew!) were only slightly higher than his ability
to dig up fifty kids who would willingly attend.

Helen didn't enjoy spending the last day of summer vacation updating her parents' Web site. Just because she didn't have a boyfriend or a blow-dryer didn't mean she didn't have better things to do.

Dear Diary:

I can't believe school starts tomorrow. Before I know it, I will be at Harvard. Though college is still years away, I have already begun studying vocabulary for my SAT's.

Dear Diary:

I can't believe school starts tomorrow. Before I know it, I will be at Harvard. Though college is still years away, I have already begun studying vocabulary for my SATs. I am not **oblivious** to the fact that diaries are **vestiges** of an earlier time. Perhaps I am a **Luddite**.

I love you, Diary,
Annalise

Marissa awoke to a self-tanning disaster.
This was so not the "back to school" look
she'd spent all summer masterminding.

Edgar knew his mother was just trying to "help," but her volunteering to drive car pool was insufferable. Nobody said a word except his mother, whose loud voice reverberated through the car like a wet cat in a trash can. It was all so depressing.

Andrew knew Caitlin Hicks was the sort of girl
who didn't know mandel bread from a matzo ball.
His mother would never approve. He was in love.

Caitlin couldn't believe Marissa was still blabbering on about her "tan."
Yes, it was very, very bad, but there was only so much one could say
on the subject. And besides, Marissa was just the sidekick.
It's not like anyone really cared.

"Where's Zac Efron, where's James Van Der Beek, where's Jordan Catalano?" Joey asked himself after passing the pathetic population of pimpled pre-pubes while he searched for his locker. And then he saw him like a beacon in the night: Tobey Diggs. Thank God.

**Despite a rough morning,
Annalise was still optimistic about the new year.**

Helen had no problem finding her group at lunch.
Cyber-camp was good, but this was even better.

"Good afternoon, ladies, I'm Ms. Patterson. I'm not interested
in your mental problems, your family problems,
your social problems, or your monthly problems.
Get ready to run, ladies, 'cause there ain't nowhere to hide."

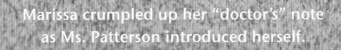
Marissa crumpled up her "doctor's" note
as Ms. Patterson introduced herself.

Cyrus was the kind of kid who spent his whole childhood having his lunch money stolen. But after being left behind for the third straight year, he was finally big enough to be the kind of kid who stole other kids' lunch money. Life was beautiful that way.

Joey hadn't realized that man-snack Tobey Diggs
was captain of the football team. Wow.
Game on, Pop.

Dear Diary:

My first day of school was **emphatically** frustrating. Call me **captious**, but the boys are **scurrilous**, the girls are **sadistic**, and my homeroom teacher is a **harridan**. All in all, the day was without the **gravitas** I had so anticipated. But, I am of a **sanguine** disposition and know tomorrow will be better.

Ciao Diary,
Annalise

Marissa was getting a stress pimple. School had barely started and Caitlin *already* had a hot boyfriend. Marissa would kill just to talk to Tobey Diggs, let alone be his girlfriend. Maybe if she lost another few pounds?

Mrs. Baker couldn't stomach girls like Annalise Glassman this early in the morning. How should she break it to her that one night of Jell-O shots and quarters and it would be Chico State and a dead-end career as a school guidance counselor?

Edgar barely recognized his mother's voice through the choking sobs.

And, of course, he wasn't allowed to ask her what she was doing in *his* room reading *his* Facebook page. Instead he was in the loathsome position of having to reassure *her* that he was just kidding about hating her, about having no "real" friends, and about wishing he'd get hit by a Mack truck before she forced him to the school dance on Saturday.

Andrew just said "hi" to Caitlin. She wondered,
did he mean "hi" or did he mean "hi"? And why was dorky
Andrew Rabbinowitz saying "hi" to her anyway?

Joey's father had been so right.
Football was fun.

Dear Diary:

What a **calamitous** course of events. Mrs. Huchel caught me writing in my journal during homeroom. I was **banished** from the class and await my **castigation** among a **throng** of **idlers, imps,** and **wastrels.** I am **perturbed** about the effect this will have on my academic record and **overwrought** at being **ogled** by the **miscreant** to my left. —A.

PRINCIPAL

"Why not let Marissa take the fall?" thought Caitlin as she let out a silent "crowd fart" and moved casually away from the table. It served Marissa right for eyeballing her boyfriend and for eating all that disgusting cafeteria macaroni and then complaining about how fat she was five minutes later.

(5u – 6v)(u – v).
Duh.
Oh G-d,
please don't
call on me...
Boner!
Omigod, omigod.
Did I just get
my period?
Joey Barontini
+
Tobey Diggs
TLF

I hate assigned seating.
Edgar Needleman
smells like wet bread.

Caitlin Hicks
+
Tobey Diggs
_____
TLF

I can't believe I got
called on. I can't believe
I said $(5u - 6v)(v - u)$.
That was way off, man.
WAY off.

Marissa got so caught up in *Cosmo's* "Rate Your Self-Esteem" quiz, she totally forgot to watch *American Idol*. Whatever. She was so hungry, she probably wouldn't have enjoyed it anyway.

That Helen should be mocked for being fat when someone like Marissa Cruz was running around free was inexplicable. Helen knew none of this would matter ten years from now, when she was an executive in Silicon Valley and Marissa was a manicurist in suburban Maryland. But it still stung sometimes.

Andrew was too busy studying his haftarah to notice Cyrus
cheating off his French pop quiz. When Madame Le-Fargue realized
Cyrus's answers were all in Hebrew, she failed him. But of course
it was Andrew who really got screwed. *Merde*.

Dear Diary:

My classmates are really an **insidious** bunch.
I try to maintain my **equanimity** but my moods
are **mercurial,** and detention is **barbaric.** You,
dear Diary, are my only form of **catharsis.**

A.

Marissa spent two hours putting on her makeup
only to have PE for second period. Ugh.
What a waste of her morning magic.

Tobey Diggs said "See you later" to Joey!
Did he mean "See *you* later" . . . or
"See you *later*"?

"Why don't you want to come over and play with him?" Edgar's mother shouted accusingly as his fellow carpoolees slunk deeper into their seats. "You think you're too good for him, you thoughtless, self-involved, spoiled little brats?"

"Jesus," thought Edgar. "I must have been, like,
Genghis Khan or Mussolini in my past life."

Dear Diary:

I think I will walk to school tomorrow. My **antipathy** toward Edgar Needleman's mother is **ineffable**. She is **porcine, gauche,** and **vociferous**. I am glad she is not my mother. The car is **dilapidated** and **fetid**. I now have an **abysmal** fear of car pool. —A.

"Do you need any maxi pads from the market?"
Helen's mother asked, as if it were no big deal,
in front of her father! That was IT.

It was bad when Tobey Diggs called Caitlin at 11:05 pm.
It was worse when her mother found out he was sixteen.
Caitlin loved Tobey. Caitlin hated her mother.
Things would end badly.

• • •

From: Caitlin

To: Marissa

My "mother" said if I ever see Tobey again she'll pull me out of school and toss me to the lesbos at Saint Agatha's. I'm taking the 11:42 bus to Hollywood. I'll get rich and famous and never give my mother a penny. Wish me luck!

• • •

From: Marissa

To: Caitlin

Don't go! What if you are abducted on the bus and get forced into teenage prostitution? Tobey isn't worth it.

• • •

From: Caitlin

To: Marissa

OMG!!!! Andrew Rabbinowitz just IM'd to ask me to be his bar mitzvah date. Is he kidding? Does he honestly think we're like equals or something?

BTW, is he really rich?

Once word got around that Beyoncé would be performing at Andrew Rabbinowitz's bar mitzvah, it seemed like the whole class came out to celebrate his spiritual passage into manhood. "Funny," Andrew thought as he recited his final chapter on spiritual enlightenment among a sea of his admiring classmates, "money actually does buy happiness."

Caitlin trampled the crowd as Beyoncé rocked the Hava Nagila.
That was *her* boyfriend!

"Life is so unfair," thought Marissa.
"Now Andrew is in love with Caitlin too?"
When would it be her turn to shine?
When would she be loved?

Madonna had to be the busiest woman alive, and yet, at fifty,
she always looked so fresh and cheerful. So why, Caitlin wondered,
did her thirty-seven-year-old mother look so wrinkled and faded?
Should she suggest Botox, or would that just get her into more trouble?

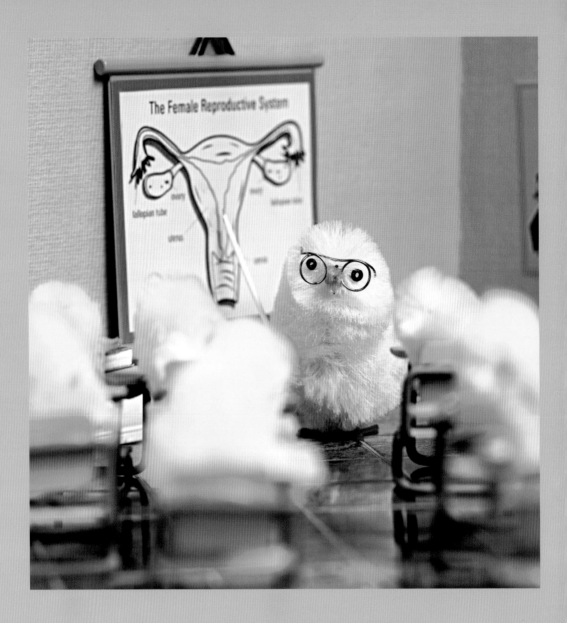

It was that dreaded time in the semester when Mr. Perez had to repeatedly say the word "vagina" to a class of teenagers. Jesus, did he hate this job.

All Annalise heard was the burst of laughter as she slammed, face first, into the glass partition. Who the hell designed this place anyway? What were the chances anyone would ask her to the school dance after that performance? ZERO!

Edgar knew the world was cruel when he was assigned
Helen Murvis as his English partner. But, as the two
reenacted the balcony scene from *Romeo and Juliet*,
the mocking giggles turned to stunned silence. They were
great. As the class erupted in cheers, Edgar knew
that things would be different from now on.
He was in love.

Dear Diary:

I am **enervated** by this horrible place. I **slog** through the halls feeling **ambivalent** about my future. School is the **leviathan** of joy suckers.

Apathetically yours,
Annalise

Gucci and Prada and Juicy, oh my!

"Another one bites the dust," thought Mrs. Baker as she eyed the narrowing distance between Annalise Glassman and Cyrus Lester. "So long SAT, helloooo GED."

Andrew closed his eyes and breathed in the sweet aroma of Caitlin's MAC berry lip stain, Bumble and Bumble shampoo, and Jo Malone Wild Fig & Cassis perfume. How could his mother not approve of such a girl? They were one and the same.

Joey was devastated to see Tobey at the dance with Marissa Cruz. God, she was sooo tacky with her bogus tan and fake Louis Vuitton bag. If *that's* what Tobey was looking for, he was SO over him.

NIGHT
AWAY

Much to Helen's surprise, Edgar gave off a spicy aroma of peanut butter and Ruffles. It wasn't great, but it wasn't bad either.

Dear Diary:

Now that I have a boyfriend, I won't have
time to study much, let alone write in my
journal. As Cyrus says, I must live in the
present and not "stress out" about tomorrow.
He is a man of wisdom.

CU L8R,
Annalise Glassman

Andrew Rabbinowitz

Annalise Glassman

Helen Murvis

Edgar Needleman